Little Blue

goes out to play

Margaret Ryan

illustrated by Andy Ellis

Hodder
Children's
Books

a division of Hodder Headline plc

For Jillian
with love
- M.R.

For Diana Klemin
with love
- A.E.

This Book Belongs To

. . . .

Text copyright © 1999 Margaret Ryan
Illustrations copyright © 1999 Andy Ellis

This edition first published 1999
by Hodder Children's Books

The right of Margaret Ryan and Andy Ellis to be
identified as the Author and Illustrator of the Work has
been asserted by them in accordance with the
Copyright, Designs and Patents Act 1988.

10 9 8 7 6 5 4 3 2 1

A Catalogue record for this book is available from the
British Library

ISBN 0 340 73986 X

Printed and bound in Great Britain by The Devonshire
Press, Torquay, Devon TQ2 7NX

Hodder Children's Books
a division of Hodder Headline plc
338 Euston Road
London NW1 3BH

It was a very wet day. Little
Blue opened the door of the
upturned boat where he lived
and poked out his head.
PLOP PLIP PLOP,
PLOP PLIP PLOP.

Fat raindrops bounced off
his beak. Little Blue sighed.
He wanted to go out and play
with his ball, but it was
too wet.

"I know, I'll try out my rain
chant," he said. "Then maybe
the rain will go away."
And he chanted...
"RAIN RAIN GO AWAY,
THEN I CAN GO OUT
AND PLAY."
PLOP PLIP PLOP,
PLOP PLIP PLOP.
The rain didn't go away.

"I'll just have to play with my
ball indoors instead," said
Little Blue.
First he bounced it off the
door. *BOUNCE BOUNCE.*

Next he bounced it off the floor. *BOUNCE BOUNCE*.

Then he bounced it off his
dad's head. *BOUNCE BOUNCE*
OWW!

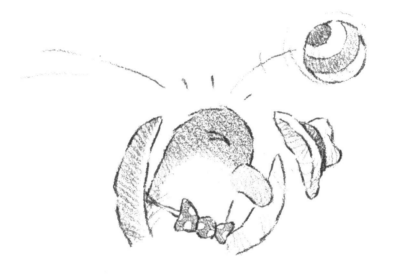

"Don't do that, Little Blue,"
yelled his dad, rubbing his
sore head.

"Sorry, Dad, it was an
accident," said Little Blue, and
picked up his ball.

He went right to the other end
of the upturned boat, well
away from his dad, and began
to play with his ball again.
First he bounced it off his feet.
BOUNCE BOUNCE.

Next he bounced it off his beak. *BOUNCE BOUNCE.*

Then he bounced it off his mum's best vase. *BOUNCE BOUNCE* CRASH!

"Don't do that, Little Blue,"
sighed his mum, picking up
the pieces.
"Sorry, Mum, it was an
accident," said Little Blue, and
picked up his ball.

"Why don't you go outside
and play with your ball?" said
his mum and dad.

Little Blue looked out of the
window. It was still raining.
PLOP PLIP PLOP,
PLOP PLIP PLOP.
"I'll try out my rain chant
again," he said. "Then maybe
the rain will go away."

And he chanted...
"RAIN RAIN GO AWAY,
THEN I CAN GO OUT AND
PLAY."
PLOP PLIP PLOP,
PLOP PLIP PLOP.
The rain didn't go away.
At that moment there was a
knock on the door. Little Blue
opened it.

"Hi, Little Blue," said his
friend, Rocky, the rockhopper
penguin. "Want to come out
and play?"

"But it's raining," said Little
Blue. "We'll get wet."

"Let's go swimming then,"
said Rocky. "And we'll get wet
anyway."

"Good idea," said Little Blue.
"I'll take my ball."

Little Blue and Rocky waddled
down to the ocean.

First they played water tennis
and batted the ball to each
other with their flippers.

Then they played water
football and flipped the ball to
each other with their feet.

13

They were just about to play a
good game of water cricket
when two dark triangular
shapes appeared in the water...
"Oh no," said Little Blue. "It's
the sharks, Fick and Fin. And I
think they've spotted us!"

They had.

They swam a little closer.

"Do you see what I see, Fick?" said Fin.

"I see the sea, Fin," said Fick.

"Apart from that, Fick," said Fin.

"Let me see..." said Fick.

"Oh I know, I see a little
blue penguin and a little
rockhopper penguin, Fin."
"You know what that means,
Fick?" asked Fin.
"It means there are a lot of
penguins round here," said
Fick.
"It means LUNCH, you idiot,"
said Fin. "Let's get them!"

16

They turned and headed
towards Little Blue and Rocky,
teeth bared and ready.

"SHARK ATTACK, SHARK
ATTACK!" yelled Little Blue.
"Quick, Rocky, dive down
through the seaweed tunnels.
They're too narrow for Fick
and Fin to follow us through."

They dived down. Just in time.

SNAP SNAP!

"Where did they go?" said Fick, snapping his jaws on a long piece of seaweed. "This doesn't taste like penguin."

"That's because it's seaweed, Banana Head," said Fin. "The penguins have escaped!"

"Actually, I quite like seaweed..." said Fick and ate some more.

Little Blue and Rocky swam
through the seaweed tunnels.
It was scary in there. Big eyes
blinked at them from black
holes. Big claws nipped at
them from black rocks. And
there was LOTS of seaweed.

Slippy seaweed, sloppy seaweed, slimy seaweed. It clung to the walls. It hung from the roof. It curled itself round and round the penguins as they swam past.

Little Blue and Rocky were
glad when they came up on
the other side. They were
covered in seaweed, but safe.
They waved to Fick and Fin.

"Bye bye, Fick," called Rocky.
"Bye bye, Fin," called Little
Blue.
"Bye bye to our lunch," said
Fick and Fin and swam away,
muttering.

Little Blue and Rocky swam
ashore to where Joey, the
little kangaroo, was waiting.

"Hi guys," said Joey. "You've
been in the seaweed tunnels, I
see. I wish I could go down
there."

"No you don't," said Rocky.

"They're scary," said Little
Blue.

25

"Can I play ball with you, then?" said Joey.

"Yes," said Little Blue. "But where can we play? My mum and dad don't like me playing indoors, and Fick and Fin are out in the bay."

"Come and play in the parkland," said Joey. "There's plenty of shelter under the trees. We'll be out of the rain there."

"Or I could try my rain chant again," said Little Blue. "Then maybe the rain will go away." And he chanted...

"RAIN RAIN GO AWAY,
THEN WE CAN STAY OUT
AND PLAY."

PLOP PLIP PLOP,
PLOP PLIP PLOP.

The rain didn't go away.

So they went to the parkland.
Little Blue and Rocky had
to hop very fast to keep up
with Joey.
They found a dry spot
underneath the trees and
began to play with the ball.

Joey dribbled it with his feet.
Rocky tapped it with his beak,
and Little Blue whacked it so
hard with his flippers, it flew
right out from the trees and
bounced off a large rock on
the edge of the parkland.

31

"OW," said the large rock and uncurled itself and lifted its

"Oh no," said Little Blue. "I've bounced the ball off Big Grey!"
"And he's there with his mob," said Rocky. "What shall we do?"
"Run!" said Joey.

But it was too late. Big Grey and his mob thundered up and surrounded the three friends.

"What have we here?" said
Big Grey.
"Looks like two penguins and
a little Joey," said his mob.
"I can see that," said Big Grey.
"And what were you three
doing?"

"We were just playing with the ball, Big Grey," said Little Blue.

"You were just playing at hitting ME with the ball," said Big Grey.

"He was, Big Grey," said his mob. "We saw him."

Little Blue tried to be brave. "I'm sorry I hit you, Big Grey," he said. "It was an accident. Can I have my ball back, please?"

"No," said Big Grey, "but I tell you what you CAN have."
"What?" said Little Blue.
"A dip in the ocean!"

And he and his mob picked up
the three friends, carried them
down to the ocean and threw
them in.

"Have a good swim," they
shouted and ran off kicking
the ball.

"NOW what are we going to
do?" asked Rocky and Joey.
"We're soaked, it's raining,
and we've no ball to play
with. Perhaps we should just
go home."

"No, wait," said Little Blue. "I have an idea. We'll go and visit my Grandpa Pen."

Grandpa Pen was having a
quiet snooze in the corner of
the big old barn where he
lived when Little Blue and his
friends arrived.

"Hullo, Grandpa Pen," said
Little Blue. "Can we come and
visit you? It's raining outside
and we can't play with our
ball any more because
Big Grey and his mob have
taken it."

"Come in, come in," said
Grandpa Pen. "I was just
having a nice dream about a
game of football. Or was it
cricket, or tennis? Come to
think of it, I might still have
an old ball somewhere. I could
let you play with it in here,
out of the rain, if you like."
"Oh, that would be great,
Grandpa Pen," said Little Blue.

"But there is one condition,"
said Grandpa Pen.

"I know," said Little Blue.

"That I don't hit you on the
head with it."

"No, that's not it," said
Grandpa Pen.

"That I don't break your best
vase with it?" said Little Blue.

"No, that's not it either," said
Grandpa Pen.

"I give up," said Little Blue.
"What is it?"

"That you let me have a game too," said Grandpa Pen. "I haven't had a good game of football, or cricket, or tennis in years!"